Discard

Arthur's Pet Business
R.L.: 2·8
Points: O.5

Arther's new
R.L.: 2·4 puppy
Points: 0.5

Arthur's first
R.L.: 2·9 sleep-
over
Points: 0.5

MARC BROWN

ARTHUR'S FRIENDSHIP TREASURY

Three Arthur Adventures in One Volume

Little, Brown and Company

Boston   New York   London

For Skye, the newest member
of our reader club

Contents

ARTHUR'S
PET BUSINESS

"You've been looking at puppies for months," said D.W. "When are you going to ask Mom and Dad if you can have one?"
"I'm waiting for just the right moment," said Arthur, "so promise not to say anything!"

That night at dinner, Father asked, "What's new?"
"Arthur wants a puppy," said D.W.
"Blabbermouth!" said Arthur.

"A puppy is a big responsibility," said Father.
"I can take care of it," said Arthur.
"We'll think about it," Mother said.
"That means no," explained D.W.

After dinner Mother and Father did the dishes.
"Can you hear what they're saying?" asked Arthur.
"They're worried about the new carpet," whispered D.W.
Suddenly the door opened.

"We've decided you may have a puppy if you can take care of it," said Father.

"Wow!" said Arthur.

"*But,*" said Mother, "first you need to show us you're responsible."

"How will I ever prove I'm responsible?" asked Arthur. "The best way I know is to get a job," said D.W. "Then you can pay back the seven dollars you owe me!" *Ka-chingg!* went her cash register.

Arthur wondered what kind of job he could do.

"You could work for my dad at the bank," said Fern. "He needs some new tellers."

"If I were you, I'd get a job at Joe's Junk Yard crushing old cars," said Binky.

"Do something that you like," said Francine.
That gave Arthur an idea.

"I'll take care of other people's pets," said Arthur. "Then Mom and Dad will know I can take care of my own."

Arthur and Francine put up signs to advertise his new business. His family helped, too.

Arthur waited and waited. Then, just before bedtime, the phone rang.

"Hello," he said. "Arthur's Pet Business. How may I help you? . . . Yes. No. When? Where? Great!"

"Hooray! I'm going to watch Mrs. Wood's dog while she's on vacation, and I'll earn ten dollars!"
"Oh, no!" said D.W. "Not nasty little Perky?"
"Isn't that the dog the mailman calls 'Jaws'?" asked Father.
"That's Perky!" said D.W.

The next morning, Arthur ran all the way to Mrs. Wood's house.
"Right on time!" said Mrs. Wood.
"*Grrrrr*," growled Perky.

"She hasn't been herself lately," said Mrs. Wood. "I'm worried."

"I'll take good care of her," said Arthur. "We'll be best friends."

"*Grrrrr*," growled Perky.

"Here's her schedule and a list of things she doesn't like," said Mrs. Wood. "I'll see you next Sunday."

Arthur did his best to make Perky
feel at home.
Every day he brushed her.
He tried to fix her favorite foods.
They took lots of long walks —
day and night. Perky made sure
they had the whole sidewalk to
themselves.

"You look exhausted," said Mother. "Maybe taking care of a dog is too much work. . . ."
"Any dog I get will be easier than Perky," said Arthur.

Word of Arthur's pet business got around.
On Monday the MacMillans asked Arthur to watch
their canary, Sunny.

On Tuesday Prunella gave Arthur
her ant farm.

On Wednesday the Brain asked
Arthur to take care of his frogs while
he went on vacation.

Best of all, on Thursday The Amazing Larry asked
Arthur to keep Cuddles, his trained boa constrictor.

Animals were everywhere — until
Mother put her foot down.
"I want all these animals in the basement
now!" she ordered.

By bedtime all the pets were downstairs.
All except Perky.
Perky slept in Arthur's room.

On Saturday Buster asked Arthur to go to the movies. "I can't," said Arthur. "When I finish cleaning these cages, it will be feeding time. And anyway, it's Perky's last night with me and she seems sick. I don't want to leave her."

"Well, I bet you're happy today," said D.W. the next morning. "You get rid of Perky and collect ten dollars!"

"I can't believe it," said Arthur. "But I'm going to miss Perky."

"Arthur, Mrs. Wood just called to say she's on her way over," said Mother.
"Now, wait here, Perky," ordered Arthur. "I'll go and get your leash."

When Arthur went back into the kitchen,
Perky was gone.
"Here Perky! Perky!" called Arthur.
But Perky didn't come.
"She's not in the basement," called Father.
"She's not in the backyard," said D.W.
"She's lost!" said Arthur.
"Uh-oh!" said D.W. "You're in big trouble!"

"Arthur, Mrs. Wood is here!" called Mother.
"Hi, Mrs. Wood," said D.W. "Guess what? Arthur
lost Perky!"
"My poor little darling is lost?" asked Mrs. Wood.
"Don't worry," said Father. "Arthur's looking for her
right now."
Suddenly they heard a bark.
"Everybody come quick!" called Arthur.

"Look," said Arthur. "Perky's had puppies!"
"No wonder she's been acting so strange," said Mrs. Wood. "You've done a wonderful job taking care of Perky, when she needed a friend the most. How can I ever thank you?"

"A reward might be nice," suggested D.W.

"Shush!" said Mother.

"Here's the money I owe you," said Mrs. Wood.

"And, how would you like to keep one of Perky's puppies as a special thank-you?"

"I'd love to," said Arthur. "If I'm allowed."

"Of course," said Mother. "You've earned it."

"Wow!" said Arthur. "Ten dollars *and* my very own puppy! I can't believe it!"
"Neither can I," said D.W. "Now you can finally pay back my seven dollars!"
Ka-chingg! went her cash register.

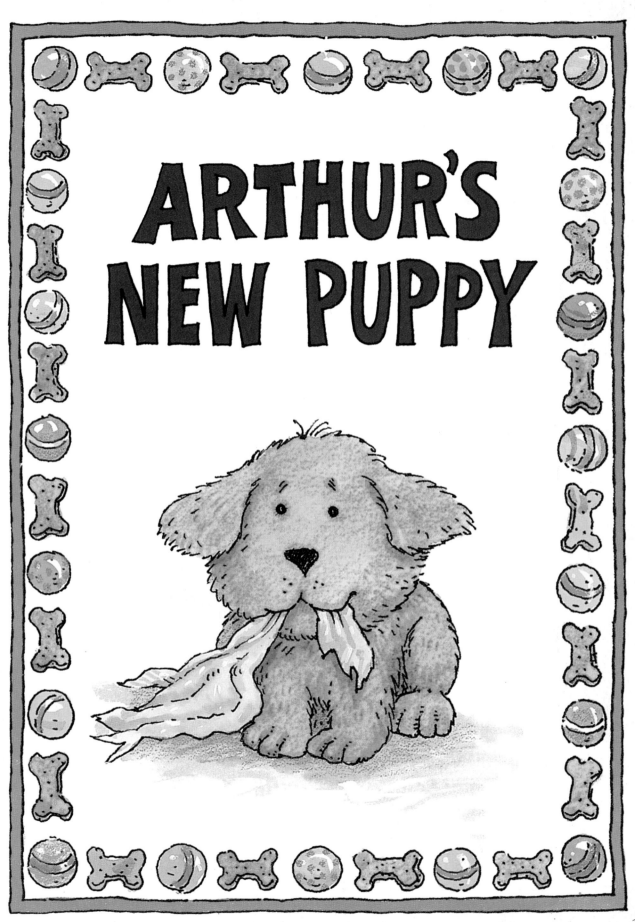

ARTHUR'S NEW PUPPY

Arthur loved his new puppy.
And Pal loved Arthur.
"He's a very active puppy," said Arthur.
"He's a very *naughty* puppy," said D.W.
"Don't worry," said Arthur. "I'll have him trained in no time."

"Here's your new home," said Arthur. "You'll have the whole garage to yourself."
But Pal did not like the garage.
As soon as Arthur put him down, Pal ran and hid.
"He feels lonesome," said Arthur. "Can he stay in the house? Please, please, please?"
"Oh, all right," said Mother, "but only for a day or two."

Arthur made a cozy spot for Pal in the kitchen.
"I thought you might need a few newspapers," said D.W.
Arthur held Pal carefully, the way his puppy book showed.
"Look, he's so excited," said Arthur.

"Look at your pants," said D.W. "You have excitement all over them."

"It's okay," said Arthur. "He's just a baby."

"Well, I think baby dogs should wear diapers," said D.W.

Later, Pal ate his dinner in a flash.
"Oh, oh," said D.W. "He has that look in his eyes again."
"Quick," said Arthur. "His leash."
But when Pal saw his leash, he ran and hid.

"I don't think he likes his leash," said D.W.

"Help me find him," said Arthur.

"I guess he didn't have to go after all," said D.W. "I was wrong."

"No, you were right," said Arthur. "He just went."

Later that night, when everyone was asleep, Pal yelped and howled until he woke up the entire family.
"Go to sleep," said Arthur.
Pal wanted to play.
"Don't forget to close his gate," called Mother.
"Good night," said Father.
"Good luck," said D.W.

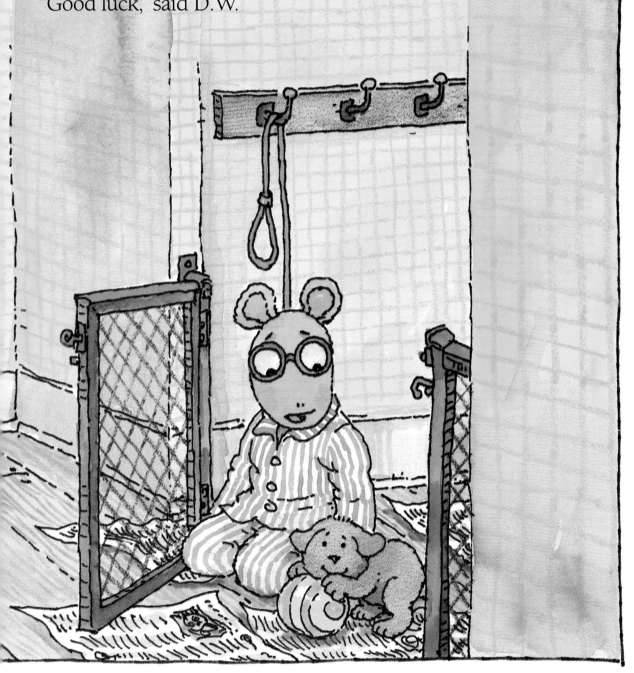

The next morning Arthur was still in the kitchen.
"Wake up, sleepyhead," said D.W., "and be careful
where you step."
"Oh, no," said Arthur, "I forgot to close Pal's gate."
"Here's your scooper," said Mother.
"You think this is bad," said Father, "wait until you see
the living room."

Pal looked very proud of himself.
"My new drapes," cried Mother.
"My doll!" screamed D.W.
"Bad dog!" said Arthur.

"Pal is moving to the garage," ordered Mother.
"Here's the key to the garage," said Father.
"I'll help you move his things after dinner."
Father put the key on the hall table.

Arthur packed up Pal's things and went to get the garage key, but it was gone.
The whole family searched for the key.
Pal watched.
"It has to be here somewhere," said Mother.
But the key was nowhere to be found.

"It looks like you can stay in the house one more night,"
Arthur said.

"I heard Mom and Dad whispering," said D.W., "and Pal's
in big trouble. They said he better be trained soon or else!"

"Shushh!" said Arthur. "You'll hurt his feelings."

That night, Arthur remembered to close Pal's gate.

At school, Arthur told Francine and Buster about training Pal. "I'm going to teach him to do all kinds of things!" said Arthur.

"I used to have a puppy, too," said Buster.
"But he was too much trouble. My parents sent him to a farm."

"My cousin had a problem puppy," said Francine, "No one could train him. One day he just disappeared while she was at school."
After school Arthur hurried home.

"Oh, no!" said Arthur. "What happened?"
"I thought I'd take him for a walk," said D.W. "But when he saw the leash, he went wild! You better get this cleaned up before Mom sees it."

"Where is Mom?" asked Arthur.
"In the backyard," said D.W. "Looking for the garage key."
"Have you seen my dog-training book?" asked Arthur.
"What's left of it is over there," said D.W.

That night Arthur gave Pal an extra training lesson.
"I'll help you train this beast," said D.W. "Let me get my whip."
"No!" said Arthur. "Dogs respond better to love."
"Watch," said Arthur. "He's getting better."
"Sit," said Arthur.

"Lie down," said Arthur.

"Stay," ordered Arthur.

"I know something he'll understand," said D.W.
"Time for your walk, Pal."

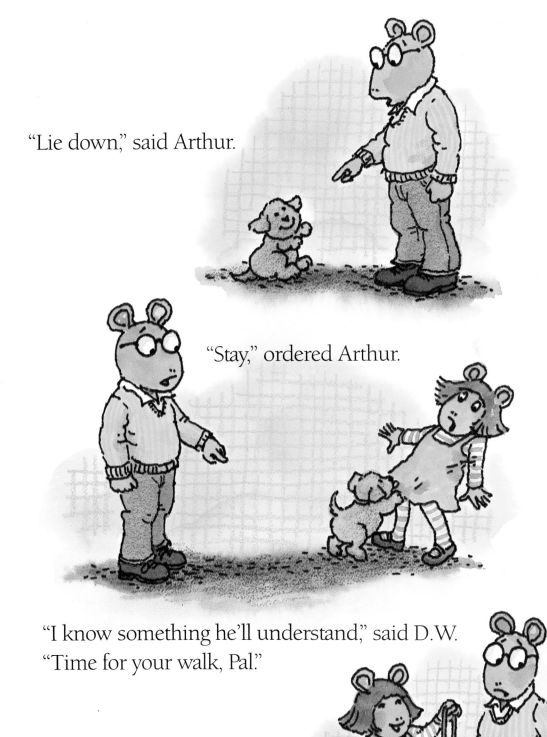

"He just needs a little more work, that's all," said Arthur.

But Pal needed a lot more work.
Arthur set up a training school in the backyard.
On Monday, they worked on "sit."
On Tuesday, they worked on "down."
Wednesday was "stay" day.
By Thursday, Pal was doing tricks.
"Good dog, Pal," said Arthur. Arthur decided to put on a puppy show for his family. "When they see how well you're trained, they'll never send you away," said Arthur.

Arthur got up early Saturday morning to give Pal a bath.
After breakfast, Arthur's family took their seats.
"Welcome to Arthur's puppy show," said Arthur. He held
his breath. "What you are about to see will amaze and
astound you!"
"If Pal amazes us any more, our whole house
will be destroyed," said D.W.

Arthur clapped his hands.
"Come!" he said.
And Pal came.

"Sit," said Arthur.
And Pal sat.

"Down," said Arthur.
Down went Pal.

Pal even did a trick.
"Good dog!" said Arthur.

"He *is* a good dog," said Mother.

"You mean he won't have to live on a farm?" asked Arthur.

"Of course not," said Father, "not even in the garage."

No one noticed Pal run behind the rosebushes . . .

... when Pal returned, he sat up and wagged his tail.
"Look, he has something in his mouth," said D.W.
"It's the key to the garage!" said Arthur.
"Good boy, Pal," said Father.
"Amazing!" said Mother.

That night Arthur gave Pal a special dinner.
"Time for your walk, Pal!" said Arthur. "I'll get your leash."
But Arthur couldn't find it anywhere.
"It was on the hook a minute ago," said Arthur.
"I know I left it there."
"I'll help you look," said D.W.
Mother and Dad helped, too.
"It has to be here somewhere . . . ," said Arthur.

No one noticed Pal run behind the rosebushes.

ARTHUR'S
FIRST SLEEPOVER

Arthur was getting ready for his first sleepover.
"It isn't until Saturday," called Mother. "Come in and eat your breakfast."

Father laughed while he read the paper.
"Some man in town says he saw a spaceship," he chuckled.
"Probably the same man who thinks he saw Elvis at the mall,"
joked Mother.
"I don't believe in aliens," said Arthur.
"Well, the *National Requirer* does," said D.W., "and they'll pay a
lot of money for a picture of one!"

On the way to school the girls were talking about the spaceship.

Arthur wanted to talk about his sleepover.

"We can have the sleepover in my tent!" said Arthur.

"You wouldn't catch me out in a tent with these spaceships landing," said Muffy.

"Bad news," said Buster. "My mom thinks I'm too young for a sleepover. I can't come."

"But you have to," said Arthur. "It's my first sleepover and you're my best friend."

"Why do they call them sleepovers?" said Francine. "No one ever sleeps."

That afternoon Arthur told his mother about Buster's
problem.
"Well, I'll see what I can do," said Mother.
Arthur crossed his fingers while she dialed.
Buster's mom did all the talking.
"Yes. No. Of course not," said Mother. "Absolutely. Good
talking with you, too. 'Bye."
Mother smiled and nodded her head yes.

"Hooray!" cried Arthur.

"Does Buster's mom know about the spaceship?" asked D.W.
"I saw flashing lights from one today."

"I think that was the Pizza Shop sign," said Mother.

Saturday morning Arthur was outside making the tent cozy for his sleepover. His family helped too.
"I was just thinking," said D.W. "How do we know you're our real parents and not aliens in their bodies?"

"Did you brush your teeth?" asked Father.

"And pick up that mess in your room, young lady," said Mother.

"Okay, okay," said D.W.

"They sound real to me," said Arthur.

Arthur was looking for his flashlight when Buster and the Brain arrived. "It was here a minute ago," said Arthur.
"I wonder if you'll see any aliens," said D.W.
"If we do," said the Brain, "how will we communicate with them?"

"Forget about communicating," said D.W. "Take pictures for the *National Requirer!* Use my camera. We can split the money."

"Let's make some signs," said Arthur.

"Good idea," said Buster. "But first I have to call my mom."

After they finished their signs, they unpacked.

"I brought a few snacks," said the Brain.

"I brought a rubber snake," said Arthur, "to keep D.W. away. What did you bring, Buster?"

"Just my baseball cards," said Buster, "and my blankie."

"Do you think we really *will* see aliens tonight?"

"No. Do you?" said Arthur.

"Highly unlikely," said the Brain.

The boys forgot all about aliens.
They were too busy telling jokes and trading baseball cards.
"Pillow fight!" screamed Buster.
"Quiet," said the Brain. "What's that sound?"
"Footsteps," whispered Buster.

"And they're getting closer," said Arthur. "Oh! Oh!"
"Pizza delivery," called an unfamiliar voice.
"Compliments of the sleepover parents."
Everyone laughed.
"I almost stopped breathing," said Arthur.
"I almost wet my pants!" said Buster.

Before they knew it, they heard another voice.
"Lights out!" said Father. "It's after nine. Bedtime."
"Already?" said Arthur.
"Thank you for the pizza, sir," said the Brain.
"You're welcome," said Father. "Good night."
"Good night," said the boys sweetly.

As soon as they heard Father go back into the house, they shot out of their sleeping bags like cannonballs.

"I heard bedtime," said the Brain, "but I didn't hear sleeptime!"

"Let's tell spooky stories," said Arthur.

"How about cards?" suggested Buster.

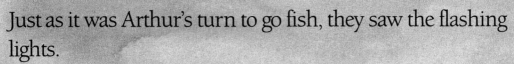

Just as it was Arthur's turn to go fish, they saw the flashing
lights.

They dropped their cards.

It got very quiet.

"Aliens!" whispered Buster.

"I don't hear any footsteps," whispered Arthur.

"Of course not," said the Brain. "They haven't landed yet."

Lights flashed again.

"They're headed for our tent! Run for your life!"

No one could find the flaps.
"Help!" screamed Buster. "Let me out!"
The tent collapsed.
That didn't stop them from making a run for it.
But a large maple tree did.
"Ouch!" said Arthur.
"I'm calling my mom," said Buster.

93

"Look!" said the Brain. "The lights are coming from your house!"
"I think I know this alien," said Arthur. "It's from the planet D.W.!"
Arthur noticed the things they used to make signs.
That gave him an idea.
"Let's put our tent back up. I think I know a way we can teach
that little space creature a lesson."

Later, Arthur crept quietly into the house.
D.W. was in her room laughing.
"What's so funny?" he asked.
"What are you doing up here?" said D.W.
"Did you come in because you're scared?"

"Not really," said Arthur. "I'm returning your camera.
You'll probably see an alien before we will."
"I doubt it," said D.W.
"Well, just in case," said Arthur. "Sweet dreams."
Then, very quietly, he returned to his tent.

A minute later D.W. heard a tap at her window.
"Aliens!" she screamed.
She screamed so loud it woke up everyone in the
neighborhood.
Everyone except Buster, the Brain, and Arthur.
When Mother and Father went out to check, the boys
were sleeping like little angels.

Of course, after Mother and Father went back into the house, it was another story.